The Very Bad Bunny

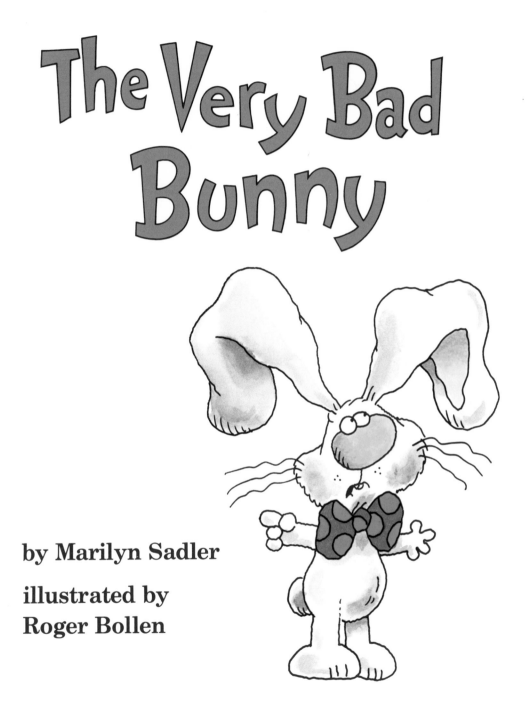

by Marilyn Sadler

illustrated by
Roger Bollen

BEGINNER BOOKS   A Division of Random House, Inc.

Library of Congress Cataloging in Publication Data:
Sadler, Marilyn. The very bad bunny. SUMMARY: The Funnybunnys all think that P. J. is the worst bunny they have ever seen, until his cousin Binky comes for a visit. [1. Rabbits—Fiction. 2. Behavior—Fiction] I. Bollen, Roger, ill. II. Title. PZ7.B635913Ve 1984 [E] 84-3319 ISBN: 0-394-86861-7 (trade); 0-394-96861-1 (lib. bdg.)

Manufactured in the United States of America 15 16 17 18 19 20 21 22 23 24 25 26 27 28 29 30 31 32 33 34 35

P. J. Funnybunny did not mean
to be bad.
But sometimes he could not help it.

One morning he spilled
pancake syrup all over
the kitchen floor.

His sister called him a bad bunny.

P. J. said he was sorry.

He did not mean to spill the syrup.

P. J. did not mean to tangle up
his brother's yo-yo either...

or cut up the newspaper

before his father read it ...

or invite his friends to lunch
without asking his mother.

"I am sorry," said P. J.
But P. J.'s mother sent him
to his room anyway.

That made P. J. so angry,
he threw his pillow out the window.
This time P. J. did mean to be bad!

The Funnybunnys could not believe it.
They had never seen such a bad bunny.

Then one day P. J.'s little cousin
Binky came to visit.

"Now, be good bunnies
and go out and play,"
said P. J.'s mother.
So P. J. and Binky ran out
to play.

But Binky was not a good bunny.
He threw P. J.'s best ball
into the lake.

Then he tossed P. J.'s cowboy hat

into a tree . . .

and broke P. J.'s baseball bat.

He even let go of P. J.'s balloon.

Binky never once said he was sorry.

"Be nice, Binky!" said P. J.
"Or I will not play with you
anymore."

But Binky did not listen.

He used P. J.'s crayons

without asking . . .

   and left them in the sun.

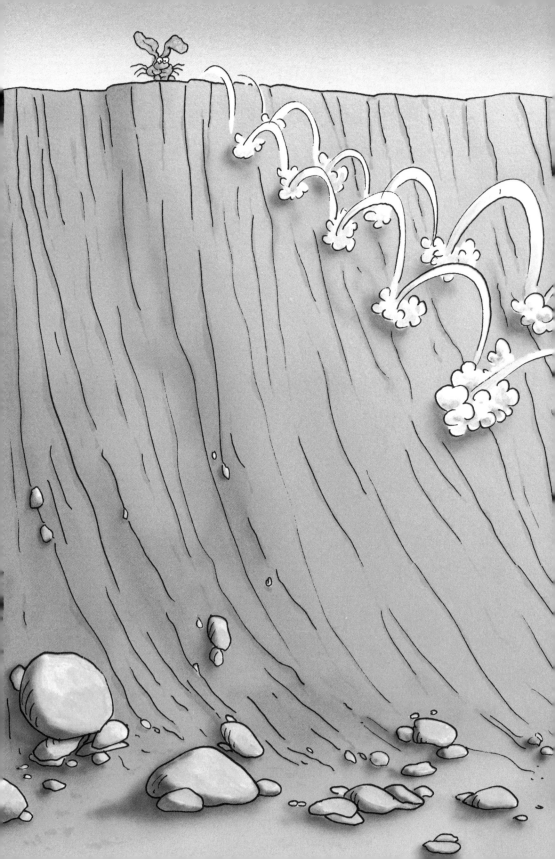

Then he took the wheels off P. J.'s bike.

"THAT does it!" said P. J.

"I'm taking you back to the house!"

But Binky was just as bad
in the house.
First he glued all of P. J.'s
checkers together.

Then he ate the last cookie
in the cookie jar.

He painted bunnies all over
the living room wall.

He put his bubble gum on a chair.

And he locked everyone
out of the house.

The Funnybunnys could not
believe it.
They had never seen
such a bad bunny.

Finally it was time
for Binky to go home.
Everyone was so happy
to say good-bye to him.

"Now THAT was a very bad bunny!"
said P. J.

And all the Funnybunnys
had to agree.